D0991862

DISCARDED
Bruce County Public Library
1243 Mackenzie Rd.
Port Elgin ON N0H 2C6

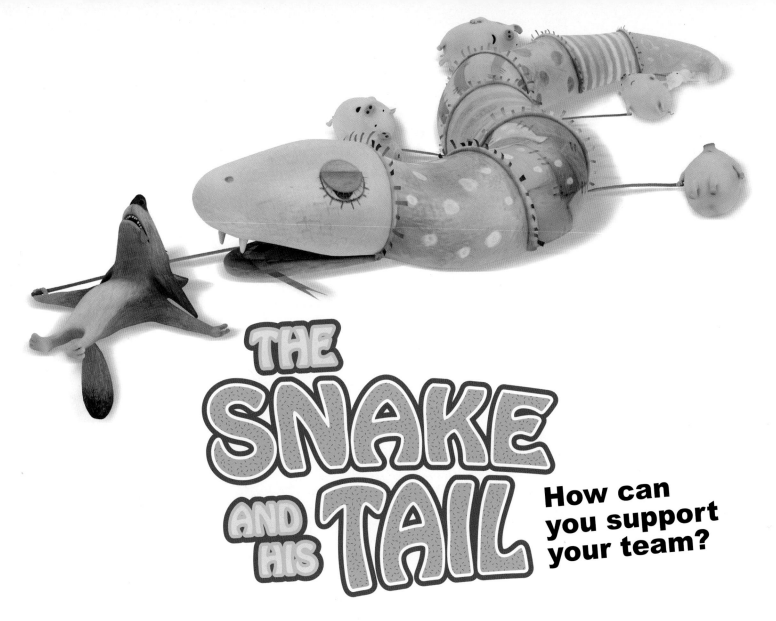

THE SNAKE AND HIS TAIL

How can you support your team?

ANIMATED STORYTIME
AV² BY WEIGL™
ADDED VALUE • AUDIO VISUAL
ADMIT ONE
POP CORN

www.av2books.com

Go to www.av2books.com, and enter this book's unique code.

BOOK CODE

E 8 5 1 9 9 8

AV² by Weigl brings you media enhanced books that support active learning.

Published by AV² by Weigl
350 5th Avenue, 59th Floor New York, NY 10118

Copyright ©2014 AV² by Weigl
Copyright ©2010 by Kyowon Co., Ltd.

All rights reserved. No part of this publication may be reproduced, stored in a retrieval system, or transmitted in any form or by any means, electronic, mechanical, photocopying, recording, or otherwise, without the prior written permission of the publisher.

Library of Congress Cataloging-in-Publication Data
Fax 1-866-449-3445 for the attention of the Publishing Records department.

ISBN 978-1-62127-923-5 (Hardcover)
ISBN 978-1-48960-137-7 (Multi-user eBook)

Senior Editor: Heather Kissock
Project Coordinator: Alexis Roumanis
Art Director: Terry Paulhus

Printed in the United States in North Mankato, Minnesota
1 2 3 4 5 6 7 8 9 0 17 16 15 14 13

052013
WEP300513

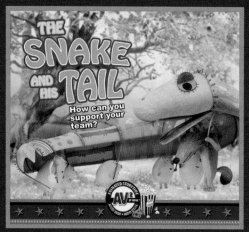

FABLE SYNOPSIS

For thousands of years, parents and teachers have used memorable stories called fables to teach simple moral lessons to children.

In the Aesop's Fables by AV² series, classic fables are given a lighthearted twist. These familiar tales are performed by a troupe of animal players whose endearing personalities bring the stories to life.

In *The Snake and His Tail*, Aesop and his troupe teach their audience that everyone on a team has a role to play. They learn that the whole team benefits when everyone plays their role.

This AV² media enhanced book comes alive with...

Animated Video
Watch a custom animated movie.

Try This!
Complete activities and hands-on experiments.

Key Words
Study vocabulary, and complete a matching word activity.

Quiz
Test your knowledge.

THE SNAKE AND HIS TAIL

How can you support your team?

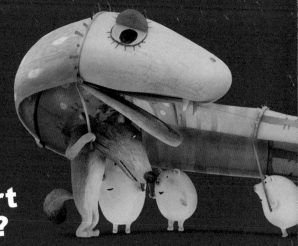

AV² Storytime Navigation

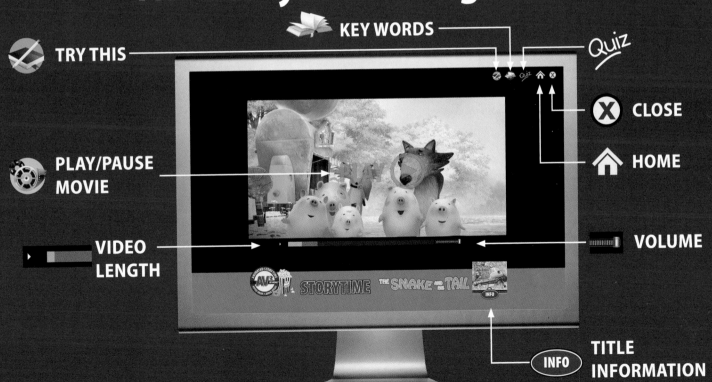

TRY THIS

KEY WORDS

Quiz

PLAY/PAUSE MOVIE

CLOSE

HOME

VIDEO LENGTH

VOLUME

INFO · TITLE INFORMATION

The Players

Aesop
I am the leader of Aesop's Theater, a screenwriter, and an actor.
I can be hot-tempered, but I am also soft and warm-hearted.

Libbit
I am an actor and a prop man.
I think I should have been a lion, but I was born a rabbit.

Presy
I am the manager of Aesop's Theater.
I am also the narrator of the plays.

The Story

Aesop was very upset.

His last play had not gone well.

"I must write a better play for tomorrow.

There are so many things to do.

Everyone is counting on me!"

The next morning, Aesop was met by his actors.
Presy told Aesop what the group had decided.
"We think Libbit should be our leader. It's about time
that we gave someone else a chance," she said.

Aesop was very sad.

"If this is what you all think is
best. Please take over Libbit,"
said Aesop.

9

That night, Libbit tried to
write a new play.
"How did Aesop write so
many plays?" Libbit wondered.
"I must make this play our best one yet."
Before Libbit could finish the play, he fell asleep.

The next day, Aesop found Libbit.

"How is your new play Libbit?"

"It's a work in progress," said Libbit.

"Well, I finished writing a play last night.
Would you like to borrow it?"

Libbit saw it and said,

"*The Snake and His Tail?*

I would have named it something

else, but it's ok for now."

Libbit gave parts to everyone.

"It's time to practice!" he said.

Libbit was very bossy all day.

He yelled at the Shorties for playing too much.

He told Aesop how to perform his part.

Libbit told Presy how to introduce the play.

"Libbit's Theater presents *The Snake and His Tail*," announced Presy.

A big snake was in search of food.

His tail bumped against the rocks as he moved.

"Hey, head! Be careful!" said the tail.

"I'm sorry. I'm trying to dodge the rocks," answered the head.

"I'll take the lead instead," said the tail.

"But you can't see!" the head replied.

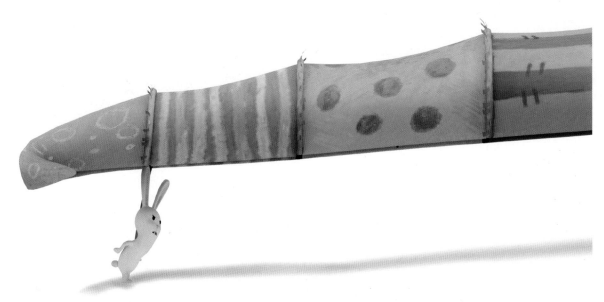

18

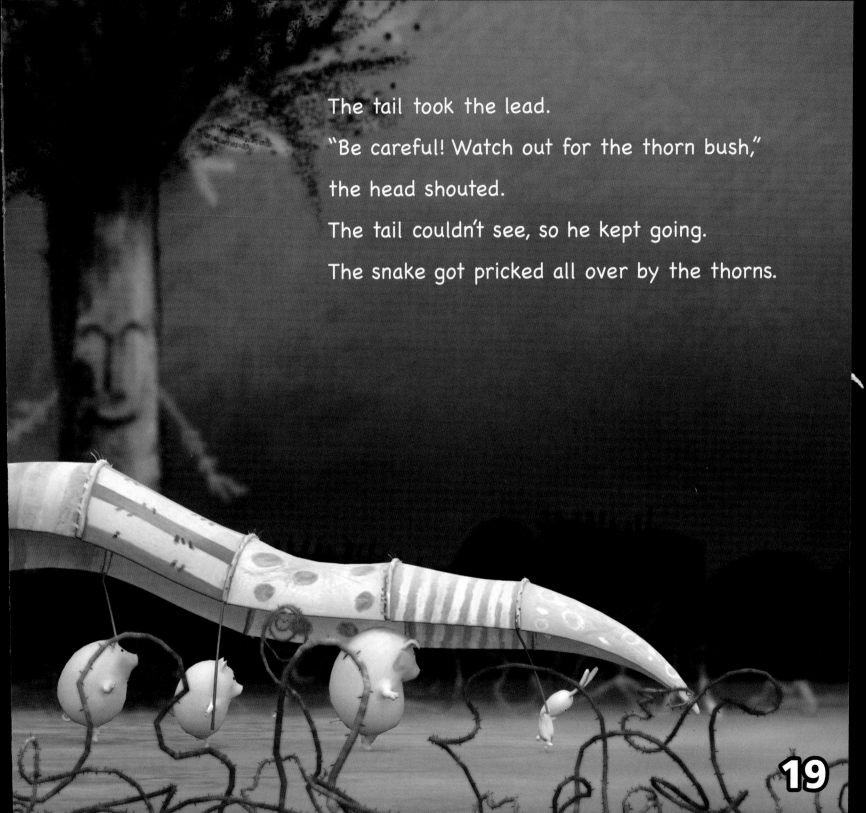

The tail took the lead.

"Be careful! Watch out for the thorn bush,"

the head shouted.

The tail couldn't see, so he kept going.

The snake got pricked all over by the thorns.

The snake made it out of the thorn bush.

Then, he arrived at a rocky path.

"Aaahh! The rocks are sharp!" the head cried.

The tail still traveled through the rocks.

The snake got scratched by the rocks.

In front of the snake was a cliff.

The tail didn't see it.

The snake fell right off the cliff.

"That hurt!" said the head to the tail.

"I guess I can't do a better job than you," said the tail.

"The head and the tail each have their roles," said the head.

The snake left for the forest head first.

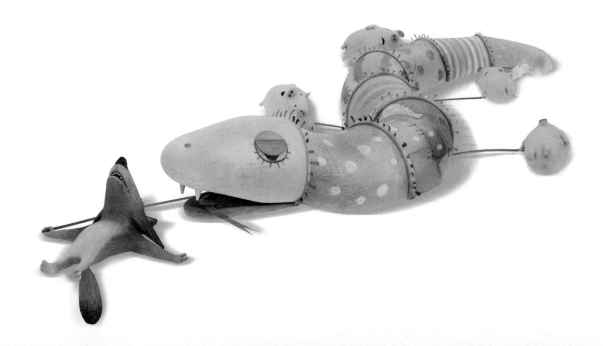

23

When the play ended, Libbit was upset.

"I could have written a better play," said Libbit.

"We're out of food. What should we do?" asked Presy.

"What am I supposed to do about it?" answered Libbit.

"You are our leader!" said Presy. "It's your job."

While they were talking, a raccoon came to see the group.

He had fixed the stage and wanted to be paid.

"Libbit is in charge. Ask him," said Aesop.

"What should I do?" Libbit asked Aesop.

Aesop shook his head.

"You are our leader. Everyone depends on you to keep them safe and fed. Are you sure you still want to be in charge?" asked Aesop.

The whole team benefits when everyone plays their role.

What Is a Story?

Players

Who is the story about? The characters, or players, are the people, animals, or objects that perform the story. Characters have personality traits that contribute to the story. Readers understand how a character fits into the story by what the character says and does, what others say about the character, and how others treat the character.

Setting

Where and when do the events take place? The setting of a story helps readers visualize where and when the story is taking place. These details help to suggest the mood or atmosphere of the story. A setting is usually presented briefly, but it explains whether the story is taking place in the past, present, or future and in a large or small area.

Plot

What happens in the story? The plot is a story's plan of action. Most plots follow a pattern. They begin with an introduction and progress to the rising action of events. The events lead to a climax, which is the most exciting moment in the story. The resolution is the falling action of events. This section ties up loose ends so that readers are not left with unanswered questions. The story ends with a conclusion that brings the events to a close.

Point of View

Who is telling the story? The story is normally told from the point of view of the narrator, or storyteller. The narrator can be a main character or a less important character in the story. He or she can also be someone who is not in the story but is observing the action. This observer may be impartial or someone who knows the thoughts and feelings of the characters. A story can also be told from different points of view.

Dialogue

What type of conversation occurs in the story? Conversation, or dialogue, helps to show what is happening. It also gives information about the characters. The reader can discover what kinds of people they are by the words they say and how they say them. Writers use dialogue to make stories more interesting. In dialogue, writers imitate the way real people speak, so it is written differently than the rest of the story.

Theme

What is the story's underlying meaning? The theme of a story is the topic, idea, or position that the story presents. It is often a general statement about life. Sometimes, the theme is stated clearly. Other times, it is suggested through hints.

THE SNAKE AND HIS TAIL Quiz

1 Who wanted to be the leader?

2 Why did Libbit not finish writing the play?

3 Who gave Libbit a new play?

4 Why was it not a good idea for the tail to lead the snake?

5 What did the raccoon want to be paid for?

6 What did the players learn?

Answers:
1. Libbit
2. He fell asleep.
3. Aesop
4. The tail could not see.
5. Fixing the stage
6. Your whole team will benefit when everyone plays their role.

Key Words

Research has shown that as much as 65 percent of all written material published in English is made up of 300 words. These 300 words cannot be taught using pictures or learned by sounding them out. They must be recognized by sight. This book contains 121 common sight words to help young readers improve their reading fluency and comprehension. This book also teaches young readers several important content words, such as proper nouns. These words are paired with pictures to aid in learning and improve understanding.

Page	Sight Words First Appearance
4	a, also, am, an, and, be, been, but, can, have, I, man, of, plays, should, the, think, was
5	always, animals, at, do, food, from, get, good, if, like, never, other, them, to, very, want, with
6	are, for, had, his, is, last, many, me, must, not, on, so, story, there, things, well, write
8	about, all, by, group, it's, next, our, over, said, she, take, that, this, time, we, what, you
10	before, could, did, he, how, make, new, night, one
13	day, found, in, it, named, now, parts, saw, something, work, would, your
15	much, too
17	as, big, head, moved, see
19	got, out, took, watch
20	made, still, then, through
23	each, first, left, off, right, than, their
25	asked, when
26	came, him, keep, they, were, while, will

Page	Content Words First Appearance
4	actor, leader, lion, manager, narrator, rabbit, screenwriter, theater
5	attention, dance, music, pig
6	tomorrow
8	morning
13	snake, tail
17	rocks
19	thorn bush
20	path
23	cliff, forest, roles
25	job
26	raccoon, stage, team

Check out av2books.com for your animated storytime media enhanced book!

1 Go to av2books.com

2 Enter book code E 8 5 1 9 9 8

3 Fuel your imagination online!

www.av2books.com

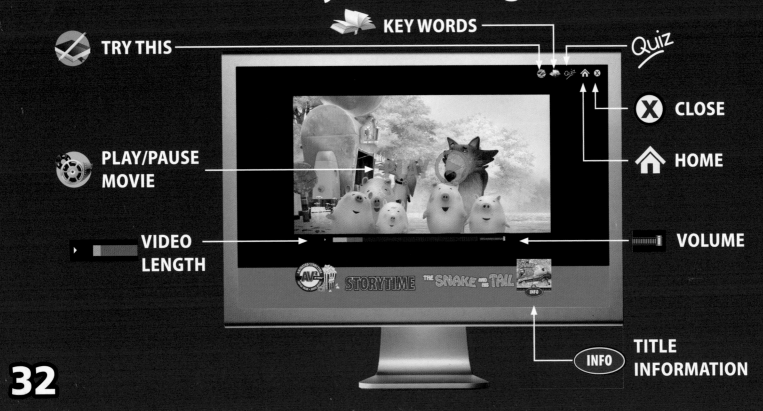

AV² Storytime Navigation

KEY WORDS

TRY THIS

Quiz

CLOSE

PLAY/PAUSE MOVIE

HOME

VIDEO LENGTH

VOLUME

TITLE INFORMATION

INFO

Bruce County Public Library
1243 Mackenzie Rd.
Port Elgin ON N0H 2C6